sniff!

sniff!

sniff!

First published in 2017 by © Rockpool Children's Books Ltd.

This edition published in 2017 by Rockpool Children's Books Ltd.
in association with Albury Books.
Albury Court, Albury, Thame
OX9 2LP, United Kingdom

For orders: Kuperard Publishers & Distributors
office@kuperard.co.uk | 020 8446 2440

Text © Stuart Trotter 2017
Illustrations © Stuart Trotter 2017

Printed and bound in Turkey

ISBN 978-1-912061-95-2 (Paperback)

Stuart Trotter

N●SY Barker

Nosy Barker
was playing with his friends,
when he sniffed a sniff, and being
a very nosy dog, off he went
to find it.

'Sniff, sniff, sniff,' sniffed Nosy Barker.

He sniffed, and sniffed, and sniffed, and sniffed into the pile of leaves...

...where he
pricked his nose
on a Porcupine!

Nosy Barker sniffed the beans...

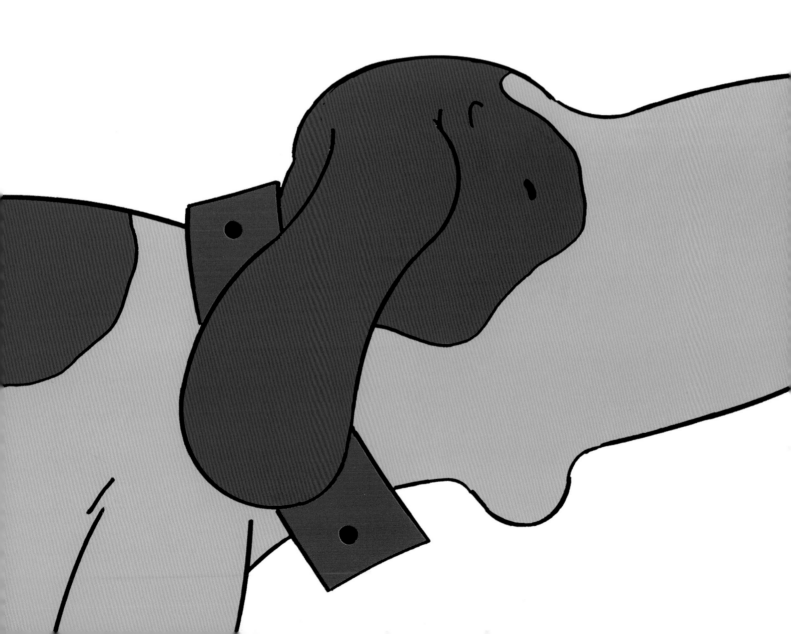

...and a caterpillar climbed onto his nose, and tickled him!

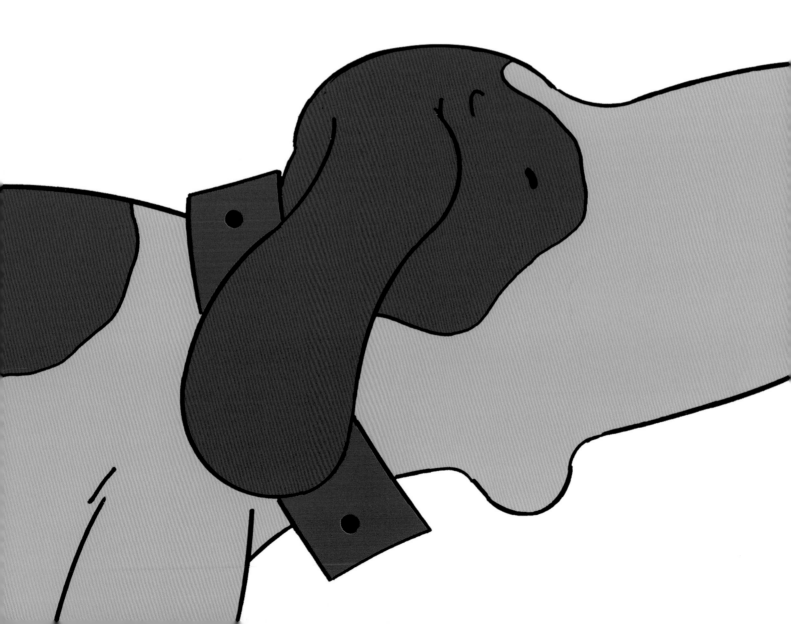

tickle
tickle

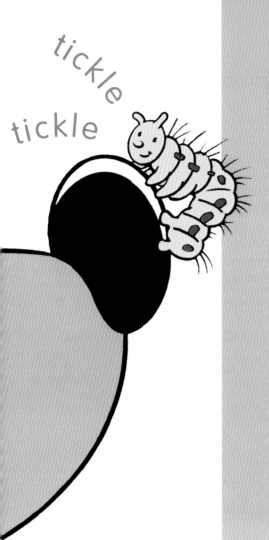

`Atchoo!`

'Bow wow,
wow, wow!'
...barked
Nosy Barker!

Nosy Barker
sniffed behind the
flowerpots...

He sniffed, and sniffed...

...and sniffed...

..and sniffed,
and sniffed...

and sniffed all the way
to the barn, where...

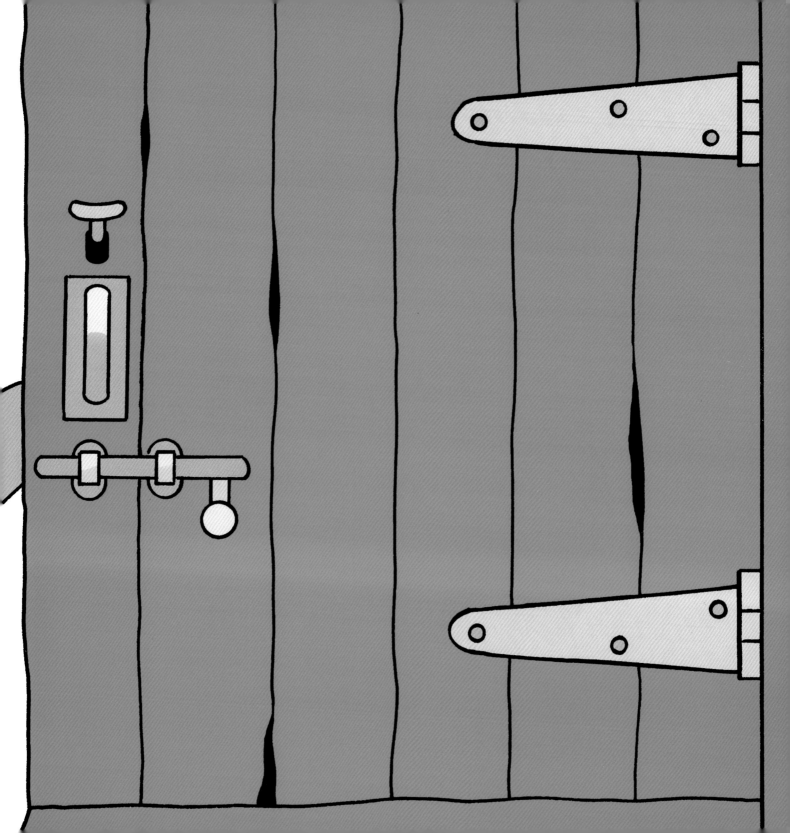

...Daisy licked
him on the nose!

slurp!

'Yuk'

'Bow wow, wow, wow!' ...barked Nosy Barker!

Nosy Barker sniffed, and sniffed,
he smelled a lovely sweet smell,
it smelled just like...

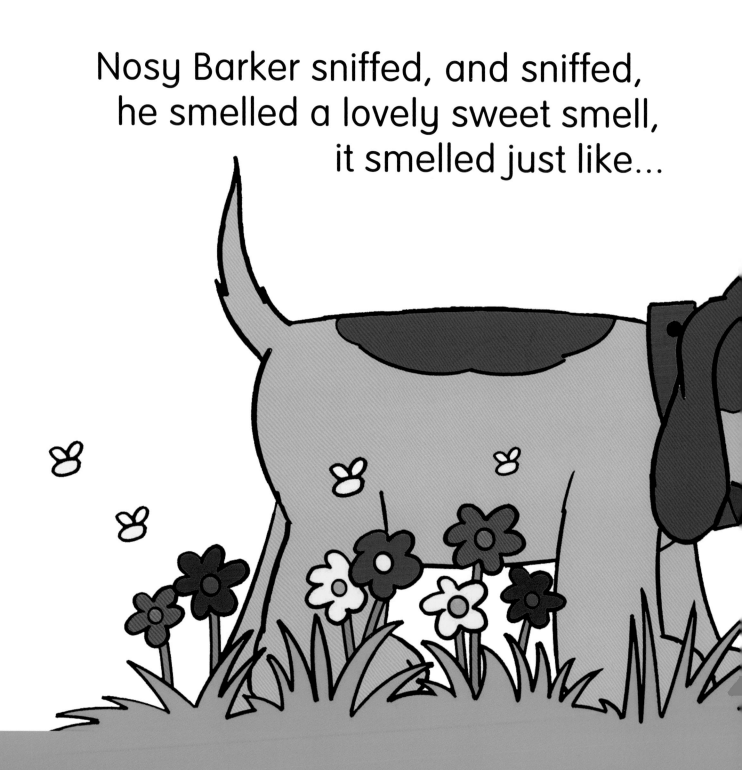

...honey!

The bees chased Nosy
past the cow....

...past the beans...

...past the flowerpots...

...past the leaves...

buzzzz z z z z z z z z z z

...and through the cat-flap,
where he smelled
the best smell of all...

...dinner!